Dear Parents:

Congratulations! Your child is taking the first steps on an exciting journey. The destination? Independent reading!

STEP INTO READING® will help your child get there. The program offers five steps to reading success. Each step includes fun stories and colorful art or photographs. In addition to original fiction and books with favorite characters, there are Step into Reading Non-Fiction Readers, Phonics Readers and Boxed Sets, Sticker Readers, and Comic Readers—a complete literacy program with something to interest every child.

Learning to Read, Step by Step!

Ready to Read   Preschool–Kindergarten
• big type and easy words • rhyme and rhythm • picture clues
For children who know the alphabet and are eager to begin reading.

Reading with Help   Preschool–Grade 1
• basic vocabulary • short sentences • simple stories
For children who recognize familiar words and sound out new words with help.

Reading on Your Own   Grades 1–3
• engaging characters • easy-to-follow plots • popular topics
For children who are ready to read on their own.

Reading Paragraphs   Grades 2–3
• challenging vocabulary • short paragraphs • exciting stories
For newly independent readers who read simple sentences with confidence.

Ready for Chapters   Grades 2–4
• chapters • longer paragraphs • full-color art
For children who want to take the plunge into chapter books but still like colorful pictures.

STEP INTO READING® is designed to give every child a successful reading experience. The grade levels are only guides; children will progress through the steps at their own speed, developing confidence in their reading. The F&P Text Level on the back cover serves as another tool to help you choose the right book for your child.

Remember, a lifetime love of reading starts with a single step!

Text copyright © 2015 by Candice Ransom
Cover art and interior illustrations copyright © 2015 by Erika Meza

All rights reserved. Published in the United States by Random House Children's Books, a division of Random House LLC, a Penguin Random House Company, New York.

Step into Reading, Random House, and the Random House colophon are registered trademarks of Random House LLC.

Visit us on the Web!
StepIntoReading.com
randomhousekids.com

Educators and librarians, for a variety of teaching tools, visit us at RHTeachersLibrarians.com

Library of Congress Cataloging-in-Publication Data
Ransom, Candice F., author.
Pumpkin day! / by Candice Ransom ; illustrations by Erika Meza. — First edition.
pages cm. — (Step into reading. Step 1)
Summary: A boy and his family visit a pumpkin patch, where they ride on a cart, see animals, and pick out a pumpkin that is just right for carving.
ISBN 978-0-553-51341-7 (trade pbk.) — ISBN 978-0-375-97466-3 (lib. bdg.) —
ISBN 978-0-553-51342-4 (ebook)
[1. Stories in rhyme. 2. Pumpkin—Fiction.] I. Meza, Erika, illustrator. II. Title.
PZ8.3.R1467Pum 2015
[E]—dc23
2014041242

Printed in the United States of America

10 9 8 7 6 5 4 3 2

This book has been officially leveled by using the F&P Text Level Gradient™ Leveling System.

STEP INTO READING®

STEP 1 READY TO READ

Pumpkin Day!

by Candice Ransom
illustrated by Erika Meza

Random House 🏠 New York

4

Sunny day.

Pack a lunch.

In the treetops
squirrels munch.

Scarecrow waves.

Open latch.

Through the gate
to the pumpkin patch!

Bumpy cart.

Ponies run.

Baby goats have
all the fun.

11

Corn fields here.

Red barns there.

Then . . .

14

Pumpkins, pumpkins
everywhere!

Jump right in
the orange sea.

Giant pumpkin

just for me.

Rolling ball.

Watch it go!

Thump!

Thump!

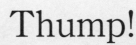

Thump!

Then . . .

21

Uh-oh!

You found yours.
What a prize!

Little pumpkin
more my size.

Take a spoon.

Scoop out goo.

Make a face—yikes!

Looks like you!

On our porch
yellow light.
Ready for this
spooky night.

Orange moon
in the sky.
Big and round
like pumpkin pie.